Box Turtle at Silver Pond Lane

by Susan Korman
Illustrated by Stephen Marchesi

Soundprints
Where Children Discover...

For Kate Mackenzie who was also born in the spring — S.K.

For Theresa and Maria — S.M.

Soundprints is a division of Trudy Corporation, Norwalk, Connecticut.

Art Director: Diane Hinze Kanzler
Book layout: Scott Findlay
Editor: Judy Gitenstein

First Edition 2000
10 9 8 7 6 5 4 3 2 1
Printed in Belgium

Acknowledgments:
   Our very special thanks to Dr. George Zug of the Department of Vertebrate Zoology at the Smithsonian Institution's National Museum of Natural History for his curatorial review.

Note from the Publisher: Please do not eat wild fruits or mushrooms. In this story, Box Turtle eats fruits and mushrooms from the garden and the woods behind the house. Mushrooms and berries may be safe and delicious for box turtles and other animals, but they may be poisonous for humans.

Library of Congress Cataloging-in-Publication Data

Korman, Susan.
     Box Turtle at Silver Pond Lane / by Susan Korman; illustrated by Stephen Marchesi. — 1st ed.
          p.   cm. — (Smithsonian's backyard)
     Summary: Box Turtle feeds, sleeps in a hollow log until near dark, builds her nest, and lays four eggs, thus completing her job as a mother.
     ISBN 1-56899-860-0—ISBN 1-56899-861-9 (micro hc)
     1. Box turtle—Juvenile fiction. [1. Box turtle—Fiction. 2. Turtles—Fiction.] I. Marchesi, Stephen, ill. II. Title. III. Series.
   PZ10.3.K845Bo   2000   00-022968
   [E]—dc21   CIP
                                                                                           AC

Box Turtle at Silver Pond Lane

SMITHSONIAN'S BACKYARD

It is early one June morning. The sun is rising over the old stone house on Silver Pond Lane. Loud quacking and honking noises fill the air as mallards and Canada geese settle on the surface of Silver Pond.

In the woods behind the old stone house, Box Turtle begins to stir.

Box Turtle slowly climbs out of the shallow bed she made under some old oak leaves and loose soil. The top of her high-domed shell is brown with splotches of orange. Her shell is very hard and strong, and it helps to protect her from predators.

Box Turtle is hungry. Slowly, she makes her way to the garden near the stone house. Her brown eyes scan the leafy plants for food. When she was younger, she ate slugs, snails, insects, and earthworms. Now that she is full grown, she also eats fruits and mushrooms.

Box Turtle finds some ripe red strawberries in the garden and eats until she is full.

9

In the summertime, the sun is too hot for Box Turtle. After her meal, she retreats to the shade of the woods. She finds an old, hollow log and crawls inside. Soon she is fast asleep in the cool darkness.

Box Turtle is resting now, but later she will work hard: The time has come to lay her eggs.

The afternoon shadows have grown long when Box Turtle emerges from her napping spot. She feeds again, this time munching on some juicy mushrooms from the woods. Then she sets out in search of a suitable nesting spot.

As Box Turtle travels across the lawn in front of the stone house, a sprinkler shoots water everywhere. Mosquitoes and gnats hover above the wet, green grass.

Slowly, steadily, Box Turtle moves along on her strong legs. Soon she reaches hard pavement. As she starts across the road, a noise fills the air. Speeding toward her is an enormous, loud machine—a car!

EXTENSION

In the nick of time, the car swerves around
Box Turtle. The driver spotted her brightly patterned
shell against the dark pavement. Box Turtle is safe—
at least for now. She continues across the road and makes
it safely to the other side.

Across the road from the stone house is a wide flower bed.
Fireflies flicker and dance among the hostas' broad, blue-tipped
leaves. A gentle breeze stirs the tall blooms on daylilies.

Box Turtle stops and looks about the garden. She
has found her nesting spot.

Box Turtle begins the difficult job of digging a nest chamber. With her powerful hind legs, she digs a hole several inches deep in the soil. Her hind legs move one at a time, first the left and then the right. With each stroke, one foot scoops dirt from the deepening hole and piles it behind her. Suddenly, she hears a noise—a rustling in the leaves. Her senses warn her there is danger nearby.

Quickly, Box Turtle pulls her tail, feet, and head into her hard shell. A special hinge on the underside of her shell allows her to close the shell tightly. The leaves rustle again as a young raccoon comes closer, sniffing the ground hungrily. His keen nose has picked up Box Turtle's scent. As the raccoon creeps closer, Box Turtle stays locked inside her shell.

The raccoon is just inches from Box Turtle when he hears a noise. Someone is coming! The raccoon quickly forgets Box Turtle. His eyes dart about in the darkness as human voices draw nearer. It is a boy and his father. As the people come closer, the raccoon scampers away.

Box Turtle hears the murmur of voices. Small beams of light dance over the flower bed as the voices get louder. Box Turtle does not move. She stays hidden inside her protective shell. Soon the humans pass by. They are simply out for a walk and stopped to admire the flowers in the moonlight.

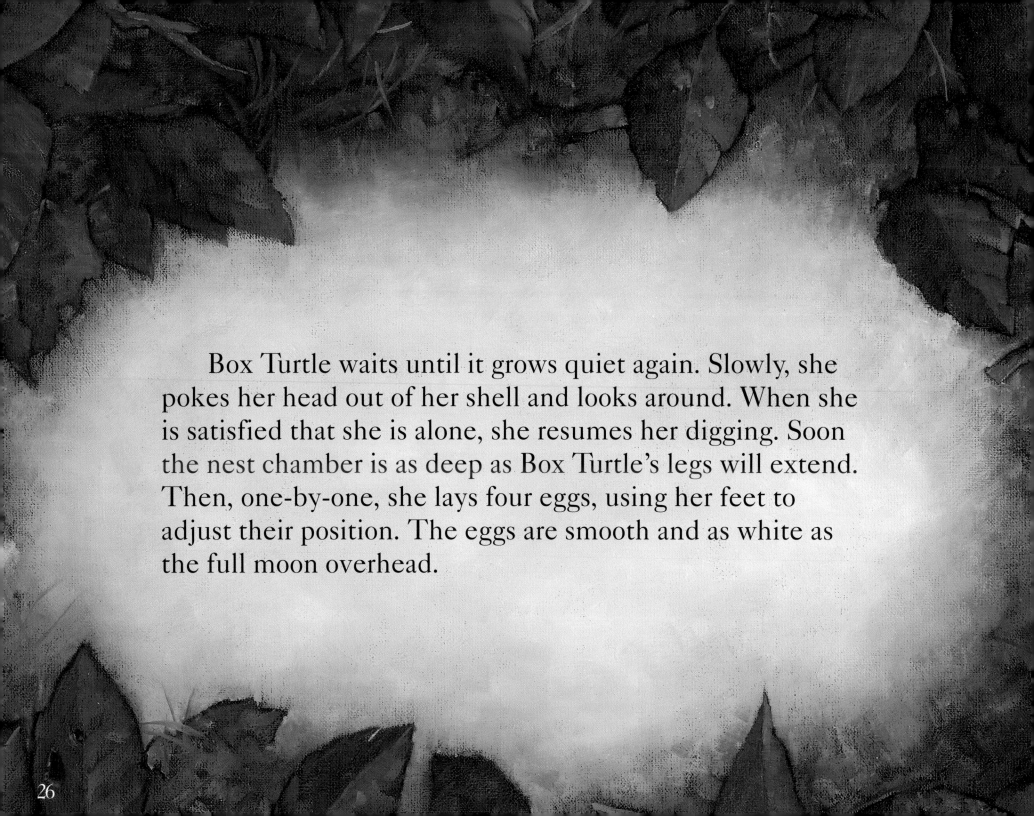

Box Turtle waits until it grows quiet again. Slowly, she pokes her head out of her shell and looks around. When she is satisfied that she is alone, she resumes her digging. Soon the nest chamber is as deep as Box Turtle's legs will extend. Then, one-by-one, she lays four eggs, using her feet to adjust their position. The eggs are smooth and as white as the full moon overhead.

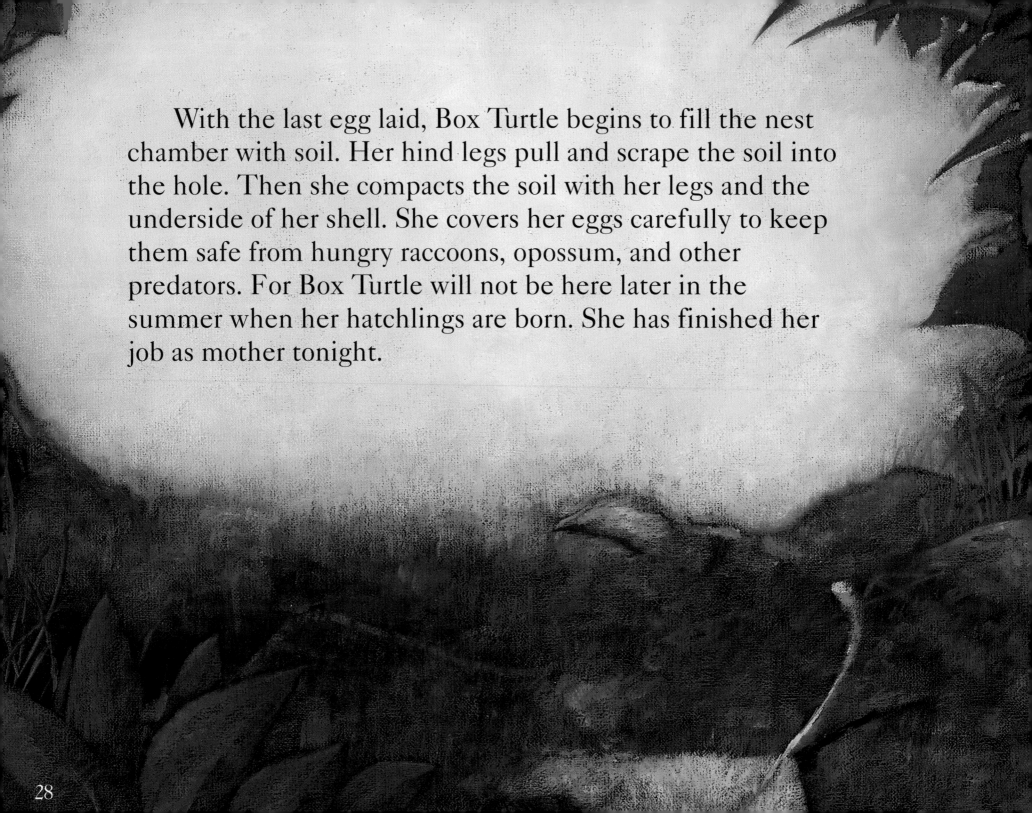

With the last egg laid, Box Turtle begins to fill the nest chamber with soil. Her hind legs pull and scrape the soil into the hole. Then she compacts the soil with her legs and the underside of her shell. She covers her eggs carefully to keep them safe from hungry raccoons, opossum, and other predators. For Box Turtle will not be here later in the summer when her hatchlings are born. She has finished her job as mother tonight.

Digging the nest was hard work. Box Turtle is tired. The moon shines high and bright as she leaves her nest and heads back to the woods. By now, the pond is still. The old stone house on Silver Pond Lane is dark and quiet. Box Turtle crosses back over the road, plods across the yard and into the woods. At last she settles down under the white summer moon and sleeps.

About the Box Turtle

The box turtle featured in this story is an eastern box turtle. The habitat of the eastern box turtle is the eastern United States. While the eastern box turtle is sometimes found near a body of water, it is a terrestrial animal, preferring to live in open woodlands.

During the cooler temperatures of spring and fall, eastern box turtles spend the day foraging for food and exploring their territory. At night they rest in shallow forms that they scoop out at dusk.

The female box turtle nests in the spring. Her eggs hatch about 8 to10 weeks after they are laid. The tiny, young hatchlings are vulnerable to many predators and instinctively stay hidden for much of their early life.

Vehicles and humans are a major threat to box turtles—both young and old. Many box turtles are killed when they attempt to cross busy roads, or they die when people take them home as pets or after being returned to the wild. Like all wildlife, they should be enjoyed where found and left undisturbed.

The eastern box turtle can live a very long life—possibly over fifty years, but most seldom live beyond thirty years.

Glossary

Canada goose: The most widespread goose in North America, its habitat is lakes, ponds, marshes, and bays. The Canada goose makes a deep honking, or sometimes a barking, sound.

hatchling: An animal that has recently emerged from an egg.

mallard: A pond duck whose habitat is marshes, wooded swamps, ponds, rivers, lakes, and bays.

predator: An animal that hunts and eats other animals.

nest chamber: A hole into which an animal deposits her eggs.

terrestrial: Living on land.

woodlands: Land covered with trees; forest.

Points of Interest in this Book

pp. 4-5: mallard ducks (smaller birds on pond); Canada geese (larger birds on pond).

pp. 12-13: mosquitoes; robin.

pp. 16-17: chipmunk; hostas (green plant on right); daylillies (orange flowers).

pp. 18-19: ladybug (lower right).

pp. 20-21: raccoon.